Dedications

To my family, thank you for your constant support, feedback and creative solutions.
To Amanda, thank you for always encouraging me to get up and try again, I Love and appreciate you more than you'll ever know.

ISBN: 978-1-949474-40-4
Edition: June 2020

For all inquiries, please contact us at:
info@puppysmiles.org

To see more of our books, visit us at:
www.PuppyDogsAndIceCream.com

This book is given with love

_____

_____

My teacher once asked me,
what do you want to be
when you grow up?

A doctor, a firefighter
or someone who
drives a big, giant truck?

So there at my desk,
I sat with a pencil and paper...

And thought long and hard about
what job I might want when I get bigger.

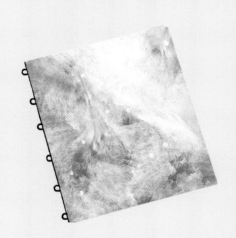

I could be a pilot
and fly higher than the rest...

But heights make me feel ill,
so maybe that's not the best.

PILOT

I could be a musician
and yell out to the crowd...

But that wouldn't work,
because I'm not very LOUD!

MUSICIAN

I could be a miner,
that could be a pleasure...

Searching day and night
for a pile of buried treasure.

MINER

I could be a engineer,
designing buildings seen from afar...

Factories and skyscrapers
that would shine like a star.

ENGINEER

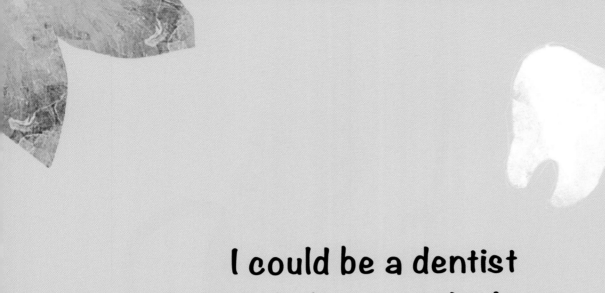

I could be a dentist
and help keep teeth clean...

Teaching young boys and girls
the importance of good hygiene.

DENTIST

I could be a fashion designer
and create fancy clothes...

With models on the runway,
bright lights, cameras, and shows.

FASHION DESIGNER

I could be a police officer,
finding clues and solving crimes...

Protecting our great city,
one crook at a time.

POLICE OFFICER

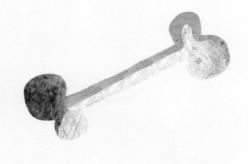

I could be a paleontologist
and discover a large dinosaur...

Although digging up all that sand
could be a really dirty chore.

PALEONTOLOGIST

I could play basketball
and shoot the winning shot...

Or trade in my running shoes
and be the team's mascot.

BASKETBALL PLAYER

I could be a photographer,
capturing animals and faces...

It would be exciting
since I'd get to travel places.

PHOTOGRAPHER

I could be a lifeguard,
it would be a dream come true...

Saving people every day
while in the ocean blue.

LIFEGUARD

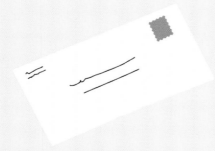

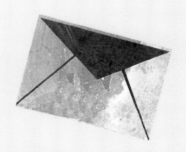

I could be a mailman,
delivering packages could be for me...

Running around and saying hello
to everyone I see.

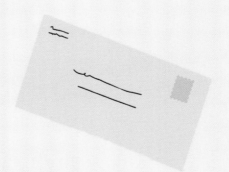

MAILMAN

I could be a tailor,
fixing clothes to fit just right...

As long as the alterations
don't end up too tight!

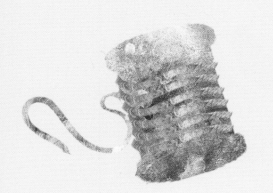

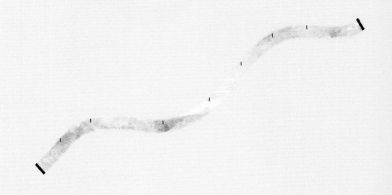

TAILOR

I could be a chef
and prepare tasty meals and treats...

Who wouldn't just love
being surrounded by sugary sweets?

CHEF

I could be a hairdresser
creating styles far from bland...

A snip here, a trim there,
with my scissors and comb in hand.

HAIRDRESSER

I could be a comedian,
telling jokes to make everyone smile...

I bet the ticket line to my show
would stretch at least a mile.

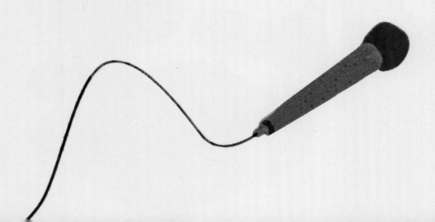

COMEDIAN

There are so many things
that I can be...

a car washer...

a crossing guard...

or a boxer on TV.

I'm still not sure about
the perfect job for me...

But no matter what,
I'll be the best me I can be!

The End